Pastor Alfred & Akiba Watts 7/19/20
May the Lord Continue to
bless your ministry as it
has been a blessing to Me
Love Your Sister In
Christ Jesus
Janice aka Sunshine

Sunshine and *Butterflies*

Dedication

To my Lord and Savior Jesus Christ who put this story in my heart and gave me the talent to express and illustrate it through this book, I am eternally grateful and give You all Glory and Praise!

Memoriam

In memory of my dear mother, Ann and my only brother West (Westi). I love and miss you both and you are forever in my heart.

Thanks

A big Thank You to all the special people that God placed in my life who encouraged and supported me throughout this journey. A special thank you to my sister, Debora (Ms. Beazy) who believed in me and put in much editing time; my dad, Wade for his wisdom, encouragement and financial contributions to make this a reality. Renee Carter, thank you for making sure I got this book started and exposing me to other authors through workshops and book signings. Thank you also to my cousin Donna St. John, Venus Miranda Perry, who's always been like a daughter to me, Angie Coleman (Sweetpea), Monica Potts (Little Lamb) and so many others who encouraged and believed in and with me that this book was possible.

Lord Jesus, may the seeds of obedience to You be planted in the hearts of those who read this book, both young and old alike. May You freshly water them every day so they blossom and flourish in every area of their lives to Your glory. Amen

This Book Belongs To:

_____

_____

Xulon Press
2301 Lucien Way #415
Maitland, FL 32751
407.339.4217
www.xulonpress.com

Printed in the United States of America.

ISBN-13: 978-1-6305-0904-0

Sunshine and Butterflies

Written and Illustrated by
Janice L. Young aka Sunshine

XULON PRESS

Sweet Pea

Westi

Little Lamb

In a small valley surrounded by lush green hills and grassy pastures lived a Shepherd named Jesus and His flock of lambs — Sunshine, Sweet Pea, Little Lamb, Bah Bah, Woolie, Westi, and Miss Beazy. They all loved to run and play, but Sunshine liked to explore. She loved discovering the delightful mysteries of nature and was fascinated by anything that buzzed, fluttered, or flickered with bright, enticing colors — especially butterflies.

Sunshine's natural curiosity often caused her to be distracted, even when Jesus talked to the lambs about the importance of obeying Him.

He repeatedly warned them about wandering off alone, mainly because mean wolves lived in the woods nearby. Wolfie was the meanest and sneakiest of all the wolves. (1)

Jesus, who the lambs knew as the Good Shepherd, always carried
His rod and staff. He used the rod to protect the lambs from the wolves
and the staff to gently guide them whenever they started to wander off.
Not surprisingly, His staff was frequently around Sunshine's neck because
her love for exploring often led her away from the other lambs.

Early one afternoon, *Jesus* was taking a nap under His favorite oak tree. While He slept, Sunshine tried her best to persuade Sweet Pea and Westi to go exploring with her.

"No way, Sunshine! You shouldn't be going either!" they both shouted.

"Sunshine, don't you listen when Jesus warns us about wandering off and running into Wolfie?" Sweet Pea cried out.

"Of course not, Sweet Pea. You know she wasn't listening. Sunshine is always off chasing something or has her nose stuck in a flower," Westi replied with a chuckle.

4

Sweet Pea and Westi desperately pleaded with Sunshine not to go, but Sunshine just ignored them, giggled, and proudly exclaimed, "Oh, you're both just afraid. Well, I'm not scared, not even of that old Wolfie! And besides, I'm not going that far anyway."

So, I'll see you guys later." And off she went. Sweet Pea and Westi watched Sunshine happily scurry away until she was no longer in sight.

Westi and Sweet Pea, running as fast as they could, headed back home. When they reached the flock, they told the rest of the lambs about Sunshine.

Seeing how upset they were, Miss Beazy calmly stated, "We must go and tell Jesus right away."

So, all the lambs ran to the oak tree where Jesus was sleeping.

"Jesus, Jesus, wake up!" Bah Bah shouted.

Jesus, now wide awake, replied, "Yes, Bah Bah, what's the matter?"

"Sunshine wandered off again, and this time she's gone too far!" Bah Bah yelled.

Sweet Pea chimed in, saying, "She tried to talk Westi and me into going with her, but we told her, 'No! It's just too dangerous.' She wouldn't listen to us."

8

"Don't worry about Sunshine. I know exactly what my little busybody has done," Jesus said calmly.

His tone seemed a little too calm for Woolie. Before Jesus could say another word, Woolie blurted out, "Well, aren't You going to go and look for her?!"

9

"Yes, Woolie," Jesus said. "And I know just where to find her. But first, there's a lesson she needs to learn. I promise you, she will be fine.

I AM the Good Shepherd, and I always take care of those who belong to Me." (2)

10

Little Lamb nudged her way to the front of the flock and whispered, "Jesus, can I go with you?"

Jesus gently patted her on the head and whispered back to her, "Little Lamb, I want you to stay to keep an eye on the other lambs until I return. That means, I'm putting *you* in charge."

Oh, how excited she was, as the *littlest* lamb, to be given such a *big* responsibility by Jesus — and that Sunshine would soon be home!

Meanwhile, Sunshine was merrily chasing butterflies and smelling the sweetness of the daisies. She did not realize how far she had gone or how much time had passed.

12

The sun was slowly setting behind the hills, and it was getting dark. Not knowing where she was, Sunshine suddenly became very scared and began to cry, "Bahhhhh, bahhhhhh!"

Looking in every direction, she didn't see Jesus, and she didn't see Westi or Sweet Pea either. Sunshine was lost and alone.

Afraid to go any farther, Sunshine laid down in the grass; all she could think about was how Westi and Sweet Pea had tried to warn her.

"Why didn't I listen to them?" she sniffled, as tears began to fill her eyes.

She lifted her head to cry out for help. But then, she saw something moving toward her in the distance. She could barely make out what it was because the sky was now dark. But as the image grew closer, it looked like Flocksey. She was one of the momma sheep that lived on the other side of the valley from Jesus and His flock. Sunshine and the other lambs would often see her when Jesus took them to the pasture.

15

Sunshine was so excited to see her. She jumped up and ran as fast as she could toward Flocksey. Almost out of breath, she could barely get out her plea for help. "Flocksey! Flocksey! Please help me!" cried Sunshine.

But as she got closer, the momma sheep turned around and headed toward the woods. Sunshine continued to call the momma sheep, but she did not answer; she just kept walking and never looked back.

By now, it was very dark, and Sunshine began to panic. She realized that she was deep in the woods and that she could no longer see the momma sheep. Sunshine called out even louder, "Flocksey! Where are you? Please help me! I've wandered away from my friends and from Je..."

but before she could say His name, the momma sheep leaped out from behind a tree and with a terrifying growl said, "You mean JESUS?" Immediately, Sunshine realized the sheep was not Flocksey, but Wolfie dressed in sheep's clothing! (3)

Sunshine was so frightened that she could not move. Her heart beat faster and faster as Wolfie drew closer. She closed her eyes tightly, as he was about to leap upon her. Suddenly, Jesus appeared and stood in between the two of them; He held out His rod to keep Wolfie back, and with stern words, He commanded Wolfie to go.

20

When Sunshine opened her eyes, Wolfie was gone.

Still shaking, Sunshine's eyes began to fill with tears once more. Jesus picked her up and held her close to Him. Now feeling safe and calm, she fell asleep in His arms.

The warm glow of the sun was just beginning to peek through the hills as the next morning dawned. When Sunshine woke up, she was still in Jesus's arms. They were now safely back home in the valley. The other lambs were not yet awake, since it was still very early.

Jesus had been awake for a while. Knowing how excited the other lambs would be to see Sunshine, He took her to a quiet place to talk to her before they woke up.

Jesus looked down at her and whispered her name. As she lifted her head to look at Him, she saw a single tear running down His cheek.

Humbly, Sunshine asked, "Jesus, is that tear because of me?"

He pulled her closer and said, in His gentle and loving voice, "Yes, Sunshine. I am hurt that you didn't listen to Me, and I needed to teach you what happens when you choose to disobey. You wandered far from all of us and put yourself in danger of those mean wolves, especially Wolfie.

He is always trying to steal My little lambs because he knows how much I love you all, and that each one of you is very special to Me." (4)

Tears began to fill her eyes again, and Jesus gently wiped them away. "Jesus, I'm so sorry for not listening and for disobeying You. Will You please forgive me?"

Jesus tenderly kissed her forehead and said, "I know you are, and yes, I forgive you."

By this time, Woolie, Bah Bah, Little Lamb, and Miss Beazy were awake. They saw Jesus sitting under the tree talking with Sunshine.

Little Lamb was so excited that she ran to wake up Westi and Sweet Pea. "Jesus is back, and so is Sunshine!" she shouted.

27

Startled at first, the two sleepy lambs quickly arose, looked over at the tree, and ran as fast as they could toward Jesus and Sunshine.

28

As soon as she saw Westi and Sweet Pea, Sunshine was overjoyed and burst into laughter.

She leaped from Jesus', arms, but He immediately called to her, "Sunshine, don't forget what we talked about."

"No, Jesus, I will not forget," Sunshine replied as she kissed Him on the cheek and ran off to greet her friends.

All the lambs gathered around Sunshine, telling her how happy they were to have her back home. "Sunshine, what happened? We were so worried about you!" Woolie exclaimed.

Sunshine told them all about her dangerous encounter with Wolfie and how Jesus had saved her.

"Wow, that is really scary, Sunshine!" Miss Beazy exclaimed.

"Yeah," Bah Bah agreed. "But we're glad you're back home safe with us!"

"So am I, Bah Bah. So am I," Sunshine said with a sigh of relief.
"And I really learned my lesson this time."

"YAY!" they all shouted as they ran off together to play.

Endorsements

Sunshine and Butterflies is a poignant depiction of a loving Shepherd's care for His lambs. Skillfully illustrated and delightfully written, Janice Young has used her God-given talent and gifts to create a wonderful book for us, young and old alike. She has invited us to a story time that will keep us amused, comforted and reflective as we embrace the divine truth of Psalm 23. Enjoy!

Renée Hill Carter
Author of "What About Me?? Staying Healthy and Whole (While You're Helping Others)" and the Award Winning A Good Work Begun.

Sunshine and Butterflies is a creative vision of how Jesus' voice echoes through His flock, bestowing the light of safety through obedience to His word. Children will immediately find themselves lost in this wonderful, unfolding saga of loveable friends who form a family, and who are clear guides through a tale of love even after temptation threatens their world. Their innocent animal instincts represent the human spirit that is often stubborn and deaf to the gentle warnings of Jesus. This story demonstrates for the reader regardless of age, that when we truly allow the Lord to be our Shepherd, we shall NOT want. (Psalm 23:1)

-Abby Flanders
National Award Winning Television Writer-Producer
Author of Fowler's Snare: Assassination and Resurrection of the Human Spirit

Scripture References

(1) You are My friends if you do whatever I command you. *John 15:14*

(2) I am the Good Shepherd. The Good Shepherd gives His life for the sheep. *John 10:11*

(3) Beware of false prophets, who come to you in sheep's clothing, but inwardly they are ravenous wolves. *Matthew 7:15*

(4) The thief does not come except to steal, and to kill, and to destroy. I have come that they may have life, and that they may have it more abundantly. *John 10:10*

All Scripture references are from the New King James Version (NKJV)

CPSIA information can be obtained
at www.ICGtesting.com
Printed in the USA
BVHW021728300620
582441BV00002B/8

9 781630 509040